LOVE IS A BEAUTIFUL LIE

SURIYA.B

Contents

Preface

Love has a way of weaving itself into the fabric of our lives, often when we least expect it. This novel is born from my own encounters with the unpredictable and enchanting nature of romance. It's a tale that celebrates the beauty of connection, the pain of loss, and the bittersweet reality of loving and being loved.

As I penned this story, I found myself reflecting on the moments that have shaped my understanding of love. The quiet, stolen glances, the heartbreak of unspoken words these are the elements that breathe life into the pages that follow. Each character is a mosaic of the people I've known and the emotions I've felt, making their journey a deeply personal one.

Set in a world where love is both a sanctuary and a battlefield, this novel delves into the hearts of its protagonists as they navigate the complexities of their relationships.

Their paths are fraught with misunderstandings, serendipitous encounters, and the kind of longing that lingers long after the final page is turned. Through their eyes, I hope to capture the essence of what it means to love fearlessly and to find strength in vulnerability.

Writing this novel has been an act of love in itself, a way for me to express the myriad ways in which love shapes us, challenges us, and ultimately, transforms us. It is my hope that as you read this story, you will see reflections of your own experiences and feel a connection to the characters' joys and sorrows.

I am deeply grateful for the chance to pour my heart out to you. May you find as much pleasure in reading it as I did in writing it, and may it remind you of the timeless,boundless nature of love.

- Suriya.B

Prologue

As the sun begins its descent, casting a golden hue over the sleepy town of Pondicherry, I pedal my bicycle through the winding streets, feeling the familiar rush of freedom and adventure.

My name is Suriya, a name my mother told me means "sun" in Tamil. It suits me.. I think, because like the sun, I strive to bring warmth and light into my world, even if it's just through my poetry; I've always been different from the other young people at my college.

While they are out chasing fleeting romance and speeding on their bikes, I found solace in the pages of the books; I read and the poems I write.

My rusty bicycle, with its faded paint and a bell that's slightly off-tune, is my constant companion. Together, we explore every nook and corner of this town, uncovering its hidden mysteries and untold stories.

One of my greatest passions is animation. I can spend hours lost in my favorite cartoons, particularly Tom and Jerry.

There's something so pure and innocent about their eternal chase, a timeless dance of cat and mouse that never fails to make me laugh.

Often, I find myself laughing out loud at their antics, even when I'm alone in my room, the flickering screen illuminating my face in the dark.

I've always been a bit of a loner, but I've never felt lonely. My poetry, books, and cartoons are my steadfast companions. Each verse I write, each page I turn, and each episode I watch fills my heart with a sense of a belonging.

Yet, a new feeling has begun to stir within me;a sense of longing, a subtle ache that tells me something is missing....

As I ride through my town, nostalgic days of my school often come flooding back. There was one person who always stood out in those memories, someone who made my heart flutter in a way that no one else ever could.

Her name was Heera.... With her bright eyes and infectious laughter, she was the first person to inspire my poetry.

Every corner of my school holds a memory of us.The old library where we used to sit and share our favorite books, the small park where we would spend hours talking about everything, and dreaming about the future.

Heera had a way of making the mundane seem magical. She was the spark that ignited my entire world.

<u>*Life often causes people to drift away from each other.*</u>

After school, our paths diverged. Yet, not a day goes by when I don't think about her.

Today, as I pedal past my old school, I decide to stop and sit on the bench where I used to sit. The soft chime of the school bell calms me, and I allow my thoughts to drift.

I pull out my notebook, the one I always carry with me, and begin to write. The words flow easily, as if the bench and the school yard are channeling Heera's spirit into my pen. I write about our shared moments, the laughter, and the dreams. I write about the ache of her absence and the hope of seeing her again.

CHAPTER ONE

MY QUIET STRUGGLE

I sat alone in the bustling school classroom, my gaze repeatedly drifting to the table where Heera and her friends laughed and talked enthusiastically.

I watched her, mesmerized by the way her eyes sparkled with joy and her smile lit up the room. Heera was the embodiment of everything I longed for confidence, charm, and the ability to effortlessly connect with those around her.

My heart ached with a deep, unspoken yearning. I yearned to be a part of her world, to bask in her radiant presence and perhaps, if I dared to dream, to one day capture her heart. But my shyness and insecurities held me back, like an invisible barrier that I could never seem to breach.

In the solitude of my own thoughts, my internal monologue played out, a symphony of admiration and self-doubt. Heera's kindness, her genuine concern for others, and her unwavering spirit had captivated me from the moment I first laid eyes on her.

Yet, the very idea of approaching her, of initiating a conversation, filled me with a crippling sense of anxiety.

"What must I do to ever be worthy of capturing her attention?"

I wondered, my eyes locked on Heera's table. "She's vibrant, so full of life. And I'm just... me...a shy, awkward boy who can barely string two words together in her presence."I sighed, my fingers fidgeting with the hem of my shirt as I watched Heera laugh at one of her friend's jokes.

I envied their effortless camaraderie, the way they seemed to navigate the social landscape with such ease. For me, the mere thought of joining their circle was enough to make my palms sweat and my heart race with trepidation.

"Perhaps someday," I whispered to myself, my voice barely audible over the din of the class. *"Perhaps someday, I'll muster the courage to speak with her."*

But for now, I can only admire her from afar, trapped in the confines of my own shyness."With a heavy heart, I turned my gaze away from Heera 's table, resigning myself to the solitude that had become my constant companion.

Little did I know that the tide was about to turn, and my journey of self discovery was just beginning.

The bell rang, signaling the start of the biology class, and I reluctantly made my way to my seat, my gaze once again drawn to Heera as She settled into a seat just a few rows ahead, her presence unmistakably drawing my attention.

As the teacher began the lesson, I tried my best to focus, but my mind was racing with a mixture of anticipation and dread. When the teacher suddenly called on me to answer a question, I felt my heart leap into my throat.

Flustered, I stumbled over my words, my voice barely above a whisper as I struggled to formulate a coherent response. A few snickers from my classmates echoed through the room, and I felt my cheeks burn with embarrassment.

Heera, seated nearby, glanced over at me, her brow furrowed with a hint of concern. I caught her gaze for a fleeting moment, andIn that instant, I felt a surge of mortification wash over me.

The thought of Heera witnessing my social ineptitude only fueled my desire to disappear into the floor.My hands trembled as I hurriedly scribbled down the notes, my eyes fixed on my desk, desperately avoiding any further interaction.

The incident had once again highlighted my crippling struggle with social interactions, the fear of being judged or ridiculed by my peers a constant weight on my shoulders.

As the class droned on, my mind replayed the moment of humiliation, berating myself for my inability to speak up with confidence.

I knew that moments like these only reinforced my shyness, making it even harder for me to break out of my shell and connect with those around me, especially Heera.

I let out a soft sigh, my gaze briefly flicking towards Heera, who was now focused intently on the lesson.

I couldn't help but wonder if she had noticed my discomfort, or if she had simply dismissed it as another awkward encounter with the shy boy in the back of the class.

The final bell of the day rang, and I quickly gathered my belongings, eager to escape the confines of the school and the lingering embarrassment from my earlier mishap in biology class.

As I made my way through the crowded hallway, my best friend, Yuva, fell into step beside me, immediately noticing the dejected expression on my face.

"Hey, man, what's wrong?" Yuva asked, his brow furrowed with concern. "You look like someone just stole your favorite book."

I just let out a heavy sigh, my shoulders slumping slightly. "It's nothing, really," I mumbled, my gaze fixed on the floor.

Yuva, however, was not one to be easily deterred. Placing a hand on my shoulder, he gently coaxed me to open up.

"Come on, you know you can talk to me. What's bothering you?"

Sensing Yuva's genuine concern, I finally relented, my words tumbling out in a rush. "It's Heera, Yuva. I... I think I'm in love with her, but I just can't seem to work up the courage to talk to her. Every time I try, I end up chickening out at the last moment."

Yuva listened intently, his expression shifting from one of surprise to one of understanding. "Ah, I see," he said, nodding slowly. "So that's what's been weighing on your mind."

I nodded, my eyes downcast. "I just don't know what to do, Yuva. I want to tell her how I feel, but the fear of rejection is always there, holding me back. I'm such a coward."

Yuva offered a sympathetic smile and gave my shoulder a reassuring squeeze.

"Hey, don't be so hard on yourself, man. I get it, talking to the girl you like can be terrifying, especially when you're as shy as you are."

Pausing for a moment, Yuva's expression brightened with an idea. "But you know, I might have a few suggestions that could help you break the ice with Heera.

What do you say we grab a coffee and talk it through?"

I felt a glimmer of hope flicker within me, and I nodded gratefully. "That... that would be great, Yuva. I could really use your advice right about now."

As the two of us made our way towards the school exit, my heart felt a little lighter, buoyed by Yuva's understanding and the promise of a plan to help me finally connect with the girl of my dreams.

Over the next few days, I found myself constantly on the lookout for an opportunity to approach Heera.

Yuva's words of encouragement had given me a glimmer of hope, and I was determined to muster the courage to at least try and break the ice with the girl I admired so deeply.

One afternoon, as I wandered through the school library, my eyes landed on a familiar figure seated at a secluded table, intently poring over a stack of textbooks. It was Heera, alone and seemingly engrossed in her studies.

My heart began to race, my palms growing clammy as I contemplated my next move.

This was it, the moment I had been waiting for. Summoning every ounce of my resolve, I took a deep breath and slowly made my way towards Heera's table.

"Excuse me, Heera?" I said, my voice barely above a whisper.

Heera looked up, her eyes widening with surprise at my unexpected presence. "Oh, Suriya!" she exclaimed, a hint of curiosity in her tone. "Can I help you with something?"I felt my cheeks flush with heat as I struggled to maintain eye contact.

"I, uh, I noticed you were studying, and I was wondering... if you might need any help?" I asked, my words coming out in a jumbled mess.

Heera blinked, clearly taken aback by my unusual offer. "Well, that's very kind of you, Suriya," she said, a small smile tugging at the corners of her lips.

"I'm actually preparing for the upcoming biology test. If you don't mind, I could use an extra set of eyes."

My eyes widened in a mixture of elation and terror. "Yes, of course!" I blurted out, hastily pulling up a chair and settling down beside Heera.

For the next hour, Heera and I pored over the study materials, our heads bent close together as we discussed the concepts and reviewed the practice questions.

My heart raced with every accidental brush of our arms, and I found myself constantly stumbling over my words, desperately trying to maintain a coherent conversation.

Despite my nerves, I couldn't help but feel a sense of exhilaration at being so close to Heera, to have her undivided attention, even if only for a brief moment.

The familiar scent of her shampoo and the warmth of her presence were intoxicating, and I found myself utterly captivated by her every word and gesture.

As the study session drew to a close, Heera looked up at me with a warm smile. "Thank you so much for your help, Suriya," she said, her voice soft and sincere. "I really appreciate it."

I felt a surge of pride and confidence, my previous embarrassment momentarily forgotten."It was my pleasure, Heera," I replied, my voice steadier than it had been in our earlier exchange.

With that, I knew that I had taken a small but significant step towards connecting with the girl I had admired from afar for so long.Though my heart still raced with uncertainty, a glimmer of hope had been ignited within me, fueling my determination to continue on this journey of self-discovery.

As the study session drew to a close, Heera looked up at me with a warm smile. "Thank you so much for your help, Suriya," she said, her voice soft and sincere. "I really appreciate it."

Emboldened by Heera's kind words, I felt a surge of determination. This was it – my chance to finally take a leap of faith and confess my feelings.

My heart pounded in my chest as I opened my mouth, the words on the tip of my tongue.

"Heera, I... I need to tell you something," I began, my palms growing clammy with nervousness. "I've been wanting to say this for a while, but I—"Suddenly, the weight of my own insecurities came crashing down, and I felt the words catch in my throat.

The fear of rejection, the worry that I might ruin the fragile connection we had just started to build – it was all too much to bear.

Cursing myself for my cowardice, I hastily made an excuse. "I, uh, I should get going.

Thank you again for your time, Heera. I'll see you around."

Before Heera could respond, I practically fled the library, my heart sinking with each step. I berated myself, my inner voice a relentless chorus of self-doubt and regret.

"Stupid, stupid, stupid!" I muttered under my breath, my fingers gripping the strap of my backpack with white knuckles. "Why couldn't I just say it? Why do I always chicken out at the last moment?"

I glanced back over my shoulder, catching a glimpse of Heera's puzzled expression as she watched me go.

The sight only fueled my frustration, and I cursed myself once more for my inability to seize the moment.As I made my way home, my mind raced with a mixture of emotions disappointment, shame, and a glimmer of determination.

I knew I couldn't keep running from my feelings, not if I ever wanted a chance at happiness with Heera.Somewhere deep within me, a resolve began to take shape a vow to muster the courage and try again, no matter how daunting the task may seem.

That night, as I lay awake in my bed, my mind was consumed by a relentless torrent of self-recrimination. I replayed the events of the library study session over and over again, berating myself for my inability to seize the moment and confess my feelings to Heera.

Why? Why couldn't I just say it? I groaned, burying my face in my hands. I had the chance, and I blew it. Just like always.My frustration with myself was palpable, my fingers gripping the sheets as I tossed and turned, unable to find solace in sleep.

The missed opportunity weighed heavily on my heart, a constant reminder of my own crippling shyness and self-doubt.But even as the waves of disappointment threatened to overwhelm me, a glimmer of determination began to take root within my mind.

I couldn't keep running from my feelings, not if I ever wanted a chance at happiness with Heera.Staring up at the ceiling,

I made a silent vow to myself. I won't let this chance slip away again, I whispered into the darkness. I have to try, no matter how daunting it may seem.

I knew that overcoming my shyness would not be an easy task, but the thought of Heera's kind smile and the warmth of her presence fueled my resolve.

I would find a way to connect with her, to break down the barriers that had held me back for so long.

As I drifted off to sleep, my mind was already formulating a plan, a strategy to muster the courage and take a leap of faith.

The road ahead would be filled with challenges, but for the first time in a long while, I felt a glimmer of hope flickering within me.

Tomorrow, I would try again. And this time, I vowed, I would not let my fears and insecurities hold me back.

Heera was worth the risk, and I was determined to prove it, no matter what it took.With that final thought, I succumbed to the embrace of sleep, my mind already racing with the possibilities that the future might hold.

THE FABRIC OF A DREAM

In the quiet of the night, she came,

A whisper, a memory, a softly spoken name.

Heera, dancing in the twilight's gleam, A figure woven from the fabric of a dream.

Her eyes like stars in the midnight sky,

A fleeting vision that makes the heart sigh.

Through misty veils and shadows deep, Her presence lingers as I sleep.

Her laughter, a melody, gentle and sweet, Echoes in the dreamland where we meet.

Though morning breaks and dreams depart, Heera remains, etched in the heart.

HEERA 'S CAPTIVATING PRESENCE

The picturesque coastal town of Pondicherry.

The sun-kissed beaches and the colonial architecture never fail to mesmerize me, but nothing could ever compare to the beauty of Heera, the girl I am deeply in love with.

Heera is the kind of girl who leaves an indelible impression on everyone she meets. Her laughter spreads joy, and her eyes sparkle with an exuberance for life.and her smile is brighter than the midday sun.

Every time I see her in the corridors of our school, my heart skips a beat and l feel as if I am floating on air.I have wanted to express my feelings to her for the longest time, but something always seems to stand in my way, turning my well-laid plans into a series of failures.

In the vibrant tapestry of our school corridors, Heera emerged as a radiant masterpiece that captivated all who crossed her path.Her contagious laughter echoed through the halls, bringing smiles to even the most reserved people.

Her piercing gaze, brimming with an unquenchable zest for life, ignited a flame within my heart, leaving an indelible imprint upon my being.Every fleeting glimpse of her sent shivers down my spine, my pulse quickening with mingled anticipation and trepidation.

Her smile, radiant as the midday sun, held the power to illuminate the darkest of days, painting the canvas of my world with vibrant hues of joy.

Driven by an irresistible longing, I yearned to articulate the symphony of emotions her presence stirred within me.

Yet, fate seemed to conspire against my every attempt, transforming my carefully crafted plans into a series of disheartening failures.

One fateful day, as Heera made her way through the crowded corridor, her laughter cut through the din like a crystalline bell. Summoning a surge of courage, I approached her, my heart pounding like a drum against my ribs.

As I opened my mouth to speak, a cacophony of voices drowned out my words. The moment was lost, my hopes evaporating like morning mist.Undeterred, I tried again the following day, but as I reached out to her, a playful gust of wind sent her skirt swirling around her legs.

Embarrassed, she stumbled, and I lunged forward to steady her. Our hands brushed, and in that brief contact, I felt a spark ignite between us.

But once again, cruel fate intervened. As we looked into each other's eyes, a group of girls emerged from a nearby classroom, their chatter shattering the fragile connection we had forged. Heera'sface hardened into a mask of indifference, and she quickly disappeared into the throng.

Minutes turned into Hours, and still, I hesitated, my fear of rejection casting a long shadow over my longing.

Time seemed to slip through my fingers like grains of sand, and I feared that my chance to confess my love to Heera would forever elude me.And then, an ordinary afternoon, as I sat alone in the library, lost in a world of books, Heera's voice broke through my reverie.

She was reading a poem aloud, her voice soft and melodious, filling the room with an ethereal beauty. Blinded by her presence, I fumbled for words, my mind racing to find the right ones to express the depth of my feelings.

But as I stumbled through my confession, Heera's eyes sparkled with a mixture of surprise and amusement.

To my astonishment, she didn't laugh or mock me. Instead, a gentle smile spread across her lips, and she reached out to take my hand.

'I've always known, you know,' she whispered, her words sending a surge of joy coursing through my veins.

And so, in that quiet library, surrounded by the silent symphony of books, our hearts intertwined, forever bound by the unbreakable bond of mutual love.

The once-unapproachable Heera had become my soulmate,

I wish this moment could last forever but every dream has a end

And as the sun began to set, casting a warm glow upon my face through the window, I knew that I didn't confessed my love to her but a beacon of light in the journey of my life is just begun.

UNSPOKEN WISPERS

Oh, Heera," my heart does sing,

"If I could give you everything, I'd fill your days with
endless cheer,

And whisper words you long to hear."

And so I love you from afar,

My silent heart, a whispered star.

In hopes that one day, you might see,

The love I hold so secretly.

CHAPTER THREE

MY DESPERATE ATTEMPTS

As I rode my bicycle along the familiar path to school, my mind was filled with thoughts of her.

I had first noticed Heera on the school grounds during recess. She was playing tag with some of her friends, and I was immediately struck by how carefree and full of life she seemed.

She had long, curly brown hair that caught the sunlight and sparkled like a halo around her head. Her laughter was so captivating that it made me smile every time I heard it.

Over time, I worked up the courage to talk to her. I would see her at lunch, sitting with her friends under the shade of a big mango tree. I would try to casually walk by, hoping she would notice me, but most of the time, she was too busy chatting with her friends to pay me any mind.

But one day, as I was walking by, she looked up and caught my eye. I smiled at her, and she smiled back. It was a small moment, but it felt like the world had stopped for just a second.

I knew then that I had to find a way to talk to her, to get to know her better.

I remember that day vividly. I had resolved to overcome my trepidation. I spent the night before meticulously crafting my opening lines, rehearsing them in front of the mirror until I could deliver them with effortless charm.

But as I watched her unpack her lunch, an unexpected nervousness washed over me.My mind went blank, leaving me staring at her like a bewildered deer caught in the headlights.

She glanced at me curiously, her emerald eyes glinting with amusement. A flicker of hope ignited within me, only to be extinguished as she returned her attention to her friends.

With a heavy heart, I turned and walked away, a profound sense of disappointment gnawing at my soul. I had failed, and the opportunity to connect with her had slipped through my fingers.

Yet, a flicker of determination refused to be extinguished. I resolved to try again the next day, to conquer my fear and express my true feelings.

And so, the following day, I approached her once more, armed with renewed courage. This time, as I met her gaze, a spark ignited between us. The words flowed effortlessly from my lips, and I shared my admiration and hopes with her.

To my delight, she reciprocated my feelings. Together, we navigated the crowded school, our laughter mingling with the aroma of fresh air.

And in that moment, I realized that the fear I had once harbored had been an illusion, a barrier I had created in my own mind.

From that day forward, our bond grew stronger with each passing day. We shared countless lunches, exchanged stories, and supported each other through life's challenges.

The mango tree became our spot, a sanctuary where we could escape the bustle of school life and just be ourselves.We spent hours talking about our dreams, our fears, and everything in between. Our friends began to notice the change in us.

They saw how we gravitated towards each other, how our conversations seemed to flow effortlessly.

They would often tease us, but we didn't mind. In Heera, I found a confidant and a friend who understood me in ways I hadn't thought possible.

We joined the same clubs and worked on projects together, discovering new interests and passions along the way. Heera had a talent for painting, and she often shared her artwork with me, each piece a window into her vibrant world.

I, in turn, introduced her to my love for music, and we would spend afternoons listening to our favorite songs, losing ourselves in the melodies.

There were challenges too. Times when we disagreed or faced obstacles that tested our bond. But each challenge only brought us closer, teaching us the value of patience, understanding, and compromise.

We learned to navigate the complexities of our relationship with grace, always prioritizing our connection and the respect we had for each other.

Looking back, I realize that my initial fear of approaching Heera was just the beginning of a beautiful journey. It taught me that sometimes, the greatest rewards come from stepping out of our comfort zones and taking risks.

It reminded me that the barriers we create in our minds are often the only things holding us back from the happiness we seek.

As I continue to ride my bicycle along the familiar path to school, my mind is no longer filled with anxiety but with gratitude for the moments that led me to Heera, for the courage to take that first step, and for the bond we now share.

Every day is a new adventure with her, and I look forward to all the memories we have yet to create together.

ETERNAL LOVE

Her smile, a gentle and endless release,

In your embrace, I feel so free, Together, just you and me.

Through storms and sunshine, highs and lows,

Our love, a river that forever flows,

With every beat, our hearts align, Heera, our souls entwine.

The world may change, and time may pass,

but our love will forever last,

For in each moment, bright and true, Heera, I am whole with you.

CHAPTER FOUR

LOVE IS A SIGN OF HOPE

The bell clanged, a jarring sound that jolted me from the daydream I'd been lost in. It was Heera. Her laughter, like wind chimes in a gentle breeze, echoed in my mind.

I was in Mr. Robert clive chemistry class, a subject I usually found dull as dishwater, but today, it was a symphony. Every lecture, every page of the textbook, every scribble on my notebook, was filled with her.

Heera wasn't just a girl in my class; she was the sun around which my world revolved.

Our love story was a slow burn, starting with stolen glances across the crowded classroom, shy smiles exchanged in the hallway, and the exhilarating thrill of a shared laugh in the library.

It was like a secret language, spoken only by us, a silent pact that made every school day a little brighter. I saw her, a whirlwind of energy and laughter, surrounded by a group of friends.

She was reading a book, a worn copy of 'Harry potter,' the same one that I was clutching in my hand.

My heart skipped a beat, a feeling I never thought I'd experience. I walked over, and asked, 'You like Harry Potter too?'

A smile, as bright as the summer sun, lit up her face. 'Absolutely! It's my favorite.' And just like that, our world collided.

In the days that followed, we discovered a shared love for literature, a passion for hiking and exploring the trails behind our school, and a natural ease that made it feel like we had known each other forever.

We'd spend hours discussing the characters of 'harry potter' during recess, we debate about the merits of Shakespeare's plays while waiting for the bus, and write each other poems in the margins of our textbooks

One particularly sunny afternoon, we were walking back from the library, arm in arm, the weight of our textbooks forgotten. The air was alive with the scent of spring, and the world, as always, seemed perfect in her presence.

We reached the park in our school, a place we often visited, where the old mango tree stood, its branches a canopy against the afternoon sun.'

Do you think,' Heera began, her voice a hushed whisper, 'that there's something magical about this place?'

I looked at her, her eyes reflecting the blue sky, and I knew the magic was her. 'It's magical because you're here,' I said, and the words tumbled out before I could stop them.

She blushed, a soft crimson spreading over her cheeks, and I felt a surge of happiness, a feeling so profound it seemed to shake the very core of my being.'

I know we are young,' I continued, 'But I can't imagine life without you. You make every day an adventure.'

Heera's eyes met mine, and in that moment, our unspoken words were loud and clear. Everything else faded away the park, the tree, the sun.

All that existed was the intensity of our connection, a love that felt like a promise whispered on the wind. That day, under the canopy of the mango tree, we sealed our bond. It wasn't a grand gesture, nothing extravagant or showy.

It was a simple promise, a silent vow to cherish every moment, every shared smile, every whispered secret.

From that day forward, our school days became a testament to our love. We'd walk hand in hand to class, sit next to each other during lectures, and steal glances across the crowded classroom, our hearts beating in harmony.

We'd even find ways to slip away for stolen moments, escaping into the quiet corners of the library or sharing lunches in the secluded courtyard.

The school days weren't always easy. There were moments of frustration, disagreements over homework, and the occasional jealous glances from classmates.But through it all, our love was a constant, a strong, unwavering force that pulled us together.

We were teenagers, navigating the complexities of life, but with Heera by my side, every school day felt like a dream. We were two souls, intertwined, our love a beautiful melody that echoed through the halls of our school.

And I knew, with a certainty that settled deep in my heart, that our story was just beginning.

As the school year progressed, we faced challenges that tested our young relationship.

There were misunderstandings fueled by gossip, moments of doubt when insecurities crept in, and the pressures of academic expectations that sometimes threatened to pull us apart.

Heera struggled with balancing her passion for art with the demands of her classes, while I found myself torn between extracurricular activities and maintaining our relationship.

Yet, in those challenges, we found strength. We learned to communicate openly, to trust each other's intentions, and to support one another through difficult times.

Our love matured beyond the initial rush of emotions into a deeper understanding of each other's dreams and aspirations.

During one memorable afternoon in the school courtyard, as we sat under the shade of a mango tree, Heera confided in me about her fears of not living up to her parents' expectations.

I listened, holding her hand tightly, and reassured her that her passion for art was worth pursuing, no matter the obstacles. It was moments like these, raw and vulnerable, that cemented our bond even further.

A PROMISE OF BRIGHTER DAYS

In hearts it softly whispers, Promises of better days,

Where kindness grows like flowers, And joy in sunlight plays.

It lifts us when we falter, It steadies weary feet, Love is the hand that catches, When our worlds deplete.

It binds us all together, In a tapestry so bright, Threads of dreams and futures, Woven tight in light.

So hold to love with fervor, In every breath and scope,

For in its gentle presence, Lives the essence of hope.

With love, Heera.

CHAPTER FIVE

"MY BREAKING POINT"

I still remember the day I first laid eyes on Heera, her chestnut hair catching the sunlight as she walked past me in the school corridor.

Her smile was like a beacon, drawing me in with its warmth. It was love at first sight, and from that moment, I knew I had to talk to her. We quickly became inseparable, spending every waking moment together, lost in our own little world of laughter and shared dreams.

Heera seemed to bring color to my life that I never knew existed, and I cherished every second by her side.

But as weeks turned into months, I began to notice subtle changes. Heera would occasionally drop hints about things she admired or wished she could do, like dining at a fancy restaurant or attending a concert.

Each time, I felt a pang of guilt—I came from a humble background, and my part-time job barely covered my own expenses, let alone luxuries.

At first, Heera brushed off any concerns I had about money. She assured me that she loved me for who I was, not what I could give her.

But over time, I started to see the disappointment flicker in her eyes when I couldn't afford a spontaneous outing or a surprise gift. I felt inadequate, like I was failing to provide for the person I loved most.

The strain began to show in our relationship. I became withdrawn, grappling with the shame of not meeting Heera's expectations.Meanwhile, Heera, sensing my insecurities, tried to reassure me that material things didn't matter.

Yet, the wedge between us grew deeper as unspoken tensions mounted.I wanted to talk about our struggles openly, to find a way forward together.

But every time I tried, Heera would deflect the conversation, insisting that everything was fine. I felt increasingly helpless, unable to bridge the growing divide between us.

One day, in a desperate attempt to rekindle our fading connection, I saved up all I could and surprised Heera with a trip to the beach a place where we had shared some of our happiest memories.

As we sat watching the waves crash against the shore, I hoped this simple gesture would convey all the love and devotion I struggled to express in words.

Instead of the joyous reunion I had envisioned, Heera turned to me with tears in her eyes. She spoke softly, her words piercing through my heart with a painful clarity.

"I'm sorry, Suriya," she began, her voice trembling. "I never meant to hurt you. But I can't ignore that we're drifting apart. I need more than what we have right now."

Her words echoed in my mind, a painful realization that despite my efforts, our love was slipping away.

It wasn't just about money it was about compatibility, about understanding each other's needs and aspirations. I felt the weight of my own limitations crush down on me, suffocating me with a sense of failure.

From that day on, we drifted apart, our conversations becoming scarce and strained.I buried myself in my studies, trying to fill the void left by Heera's absence.

Each passing day felt like a battle against the memories of what once was, against the hollow ache of a love that couldn't withstand the tests of circumstance and expectation.

In this revised version, the focus is on the emotional turmoil and the gradual unraveling of their relationship due to mismatched expectations and unspoken frustrations, rather than solely on material wealth.

It highlights the complexities of relationships and the poignant realization that love alone cannot always conquer all obstacles.

A FLICKER IN THE DARK

"Suriya, do you ever think about the future? About what comes next?"

I take a deep breath, my mind racing.

"I do, Heera. And I know that whatever the future holds,

I want you to be a part of it.

"She smiles, a tear escaping her eye. "I feel the same way."

After all it just a Lie

Is it love, or just the game? A fleeting spark without a flame.

I seek the truth in every glance, Hoping for a chance of romance.

CHAPTER SIX

"MY TURNING POINT"

I remember the day Heera broke up with me like it was yesterday. We were sitting in our favorite spot in the school courtyard, a secluded bench nestled between two towering mango trees.

The leaves were just starting to turn, a riot of oranges and yellows that should have been a beautiful backdrop to our conversation. Instead, I was drowning in my own thoughts and feelings, trying to make sense of the words that had just come out of Heera's mouth."

I can't do this anymore, Suriya," she had said, her voice quiet but firm. "I care about you, but I don't think we're right for each other."

I had stared at her for a long moment, my mind racing. This had come out of nowhere, or so it seemed to me. We had been together for over a year, and things had been going well. Or so I had thought.

But as the days turned into weeks, and the weeks into months, I realized that Heera had been distancing herself from me.

She had been busy with school and extracurricular activities, and I had told myself that was why she had been spending less and less time with me.

Now, as I sat alone on that bench, I knew that wasn't the case. Heera had been trying to tell me something, and I had been too blind to see it.

The days that followed were a blur. I wandered the halls of the school like a ghost, trying to avoid the pitying looks of my classmates. Concentration eluded me, my mind always drifting back to Heera and the abrupt end of our relationship.

One particularly bleak afternoon, I found myself sitting in the library, staring blankly at a textbook. The words on the page made no sense to me.

I closed the book with a sigh, running a hand through my hair. I needed to talk to someone, to try and make sense of what had happened.

So I reached out to my best friend, Yuva."Can we talk?" I asked him after class.

He nodded, sensing the gravity in my voice.

We found a quiet corner in the library, away from prying eyes. I hesitated, then finally poured out everything that had been weighing on my heart."

I don't know what to do, Yuva," I admitted, my voice barely above a whisper.

"I miss her so much, but I don't know how to fix things. I don't even know if I want to."Yuva listened patiently, his expression sympathetic.

"It's okay to feel this way, Suriya," he said.

"Breakups are hard, and it's normal to feel lost and confused. But you need to give yourself time to heal. And maybe, in time, you'll be able to see things more clearly."

I knew he was right, but it was hard to accept. I wanted to fix things with Heera, to go back to the way things were before. But deep down, I knew that wasn't possible.

As the days turned into weeks, I tried to shift my focus. I buried myself in my schoolwork, hoping the distraction would help.

I started spending more time with my classmates, making an effort to be more social. Gradually, I found a new rhythm to my life.

One afternoon, I was sitting in the courtyard again, this time with Yuva and a few other friends. We were laughing about something trivial when I suddenly realized I was enjoying myself.

The ache in my heart was still there, but it was less intense, more bearable.Later that evening, as I lay in bed, I thought about Heera. I still missed her, but the sharp pain of loss had dulled.

Yuva's words echoed in my mind:*"Give yourself time to heal."*

He had been right. Healing took time, and I was starting to see that now. I didn't have all the answers, but I was beginning to accept that it was okay. I was starting to heal, starting to move on.

Life wasn't the same without Heera, but it was okay. And for now, that was enough.

I used to chase love, beg and plead, A heart laid bare in desperate need, But found each time, it slipped away, Like water through my hands of clay.

Now I search for something more, Not the wild flames that burn and roar, But a steady light, a gentle hand, A soul that seeks to understand.

In conversations, quiet, deep, Where secrets stir and shadows creep, I find a place where I can be, My true self, unmasked and free.

No more tears for love untrue, No more hearts that break in two, Just simple moments, shared and real, A knowing glance, the warmth we feel.For love that's begged is often weak, But understanding, that's what I seek, A bond that's built on trust and care, A love that's honest, pure, and rare.

So now I rode my bicycle in this winding road, With a lighter heart, a lighter load, Seeking not to be adored, But to be heard, and understood.

MY TURNING POINT

In shadows deep, I wanderd lost, A soul adrift, at heavy cost.

whispers of doubt, a storm within, A fight with fear, a quest to win.

A spark ignites,a sudden flare, darkness shatterd,light laid bare.

Heartbeats quicken, courage found.From trembling knees, i rise unbound.

A line is crossed,a choice is made.In destiny's hand my fears now fade.

With fierce resolve, i claim my right, In the turning point, I find my light.

CHAPTER SEVEN

THE NEW BEGINNING

I was lost for a while after the COVID-19 lockdown. I stumbled through my days in a daze, going through the motions but never truly present. I couldn't focus on anything and couldn't find pleasure in the activities that once brought me joy.

Each day felt like a blur, blending into the next with no clear purpose or direction.

The hobbies and interests that used to excite me now felt meaningless, and I struggled to find motivation or satisfaction in my daily routine. It was as if a fog had settled over my mind, leaving me disconnected from the world around me and from myself.

My heart was a gaping wound, and I wasn't sure how to heal it.

It was autumn when everything fell apart, the trees shedding their leaves as I shed my old life. The streets seemed emptier, my house colder. The books that once provided solace now felt heavy and distant.

I avoided friends, their well meaning sympathy only deepening my sense of isolation.

But eventually, I realized that I had to move on.

I couldn't let the pain of my breakup consume me forever. I needed to find a way to pick up the pieces and start living again. The video featured a nurse sharing her story of compassion, resilience, and the profound impact she had on her patients' lives. As I watched, I was moved by her dedication and the sense of purpose she conveyed.

I realized that nursing wasn't just a career; it was a calling, a way to make a meaningful difference in the world.

In that moment, something within me shifted. I felt a spark of inspiration, a glimmer of hope that I hadn't felt in months. The idea of becoming a nurse began to take root in my mind, filling me with a newfound sense of direction.

I imagined myself in a hospital setting, comforting patients, providing care, and contributing to their recovery. The thought was both daunting and exhilarating.

I needed to do something that could also help me find myself again. With a deep breath, I filled out the application and I submitted.

The first few months were grueling. I was constantly exhausted, both physically and emotionally.The coursework was rigorous, the hours long. Anatomy, physiology, pharmacology—the sheer volume of information was overwhelming.

I found myself staying up late into the night, poring over textbooks until the words blurred together.

There were times when I felt like giving up, when the weight of my past and the pressure of the present seemed too much to bear.

One particularly tough evening, I found myself in the college library, surrounded by books and notes, feeling utterly defeated. My eyes burned from lack of sleep, my mind foggy with fatigue.

I closed my eyes, wondering if I had made a mistake. But then I remembered why I had started this journey in the first place.

I thought about the kind of nurse I wanted to be, the kind of person who could bring comfort and care to those in need. I took a deep breath, opened my eyes, and dove back into my studies.

Gradually, things began to change. I started to feel a sense of purpose again. I loved learning about the human body, the intricate systems that kept us alive and functioning.

I marveled at the resilience of the human spirit, at the strength people could find in the face of illness and adversity.

The first time a patient smiled at me, genuinely grateful for my help, it felt like a balm to my wounded heart.

In nursing college I also found a new family. My classmates Jeeva, Tamil, Shakti, Rinu and I bonded over shared struggles and triumphs.

We formed study groups, quizzing each other on medical terminology and procedures. We laughed together, cried together, and supported each other through the ups and downs of our training.

Rinu, with her cringe laughter, became my closest friend. Jeeva, who always had a word of encouragement, was like a small brother. They made the long days and nights bearable, and I knew I could always count on them.

There were moments of doubt, of course. Times when I questioned my decision, when the ghosts of my past threatened to pull me back into the darkness.But each time, I reminded myself of the journey I was on. I thought of the patients who needed me, of the lives I could touch.

Slowly but surely, I began to heal.

By the end of my second year, I was a different person. I had found strength I didn't know I possessed, resilience I hadn't realized I was capable of.I was still a work in progress, still mending the pieces of my heart, but I was moving forward. Nursing had given me a new sense of purpose, a new direction.

And as I stood at the beginning of my Third year, looking ahead at the challenges and opportunities to come, I felt something I hadn't felt in a long time hope.

I knew that there would be difficult days ahead, moments of doubt and struggle. But I also knew that I was on the right path, that I was exactly where I was meant to be.

And for the first time in a long time, I was excited about the future.The sun dips lower in the sky, casting long shadows across the schoolyard. I close my notebook and sit quietly, feeling a mix of melancholy and contentment.

Though Heera is no longer part of my everyday life, she remains a vital part of my memories and my poetry. And as long as I have my words, I know I am never truly alone.

56

Healing After Heartbreak

Breakups can be incredibly painful, and it's completely normal to feel a mix of emotions.

Remember, healing is a process and it's perfectly okay to take all the time you need.

Surround yourself with people who care about you and bring positivity into your life.

Don't hesitate to lean on friends and family; they want to help you through this.

It's also important to take care of yourself—do things that you enjoy, keep active, and maybe even try something new that you've always wanted to explore.

Your worth is not defined by this relationship, and brighter days are ahead, even if it doesn't feel that way right now.

You're stronger than you think, and with time, this pain will become more manageable.

Our life is like my rusty cycle, With two pedals—good and bad times. Sometimes we need to balance both, And ride through hills and climb.

The good times bring a breeze of joy, A ride on smooth, untroubled roads. The sun is bright, the path is clear, No burdens, lightened loads.

But then the bad times clank and grind, Like rusty gears that creak with age. We struggle up the steeper slopes, And face the storm's fierce rage.

Yet both these pedals, worn and true, Are part of our life's long ride. In balancing their push and pull, We find our strength inside.

So pedal on through thick and thin, For each rough patch will pass. Embrace the journey, rusty cycle, And pedal with heart steadfast.

With this suriya signing off..........